A LETTER FOR BEAR

DAVID LUCAS

Bear was a postman.
There were always lots of letters to deliver.

But there were never any
letters for Bear.

Bear always delivered letters
to the right address.

But no one seemed to notice Bear at all.

And every day,
when his bag was empty,
Bear set off back to his cave...

...where he hung up his hat and
cooked some soup and thought
about what it would be like to
get a letter one day.

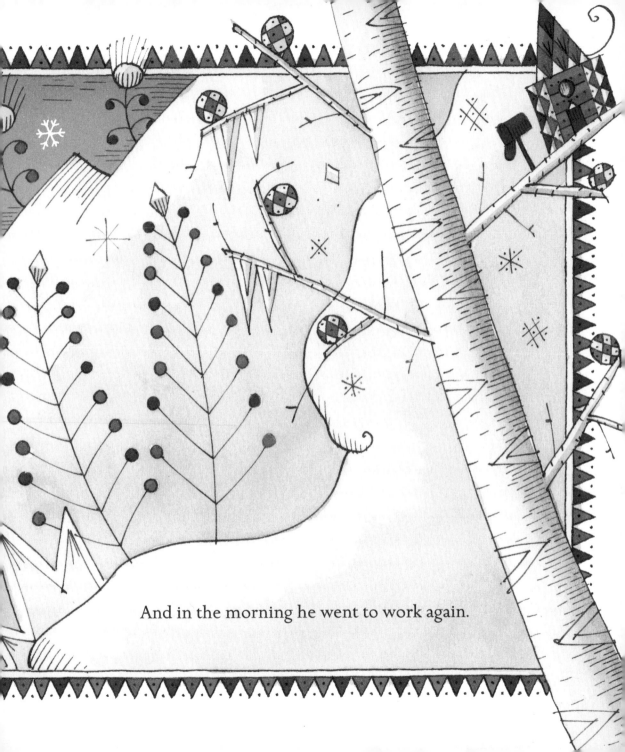

And in the morning he went to work again.

But that day the wind blew
all the letters high in the air.

And when, at last, he'd gathered
them all up, every address
was smudged.

So he had to knock on every door to be sure he had the right address. And that was how he got to know every creature by name.

And he saw each family together
in the warm and he felt lonely
in a way he never had before.

And when his bag was empty,
Bear set off back to his cave...

...where he hung up his hat,
and cooked some soup, and stared at the night.

But as he looked out at the falling
snow, he had an idea.
He began to write a letter.
Not just one letter - lots of letters -
a whole snowstorm of letters.

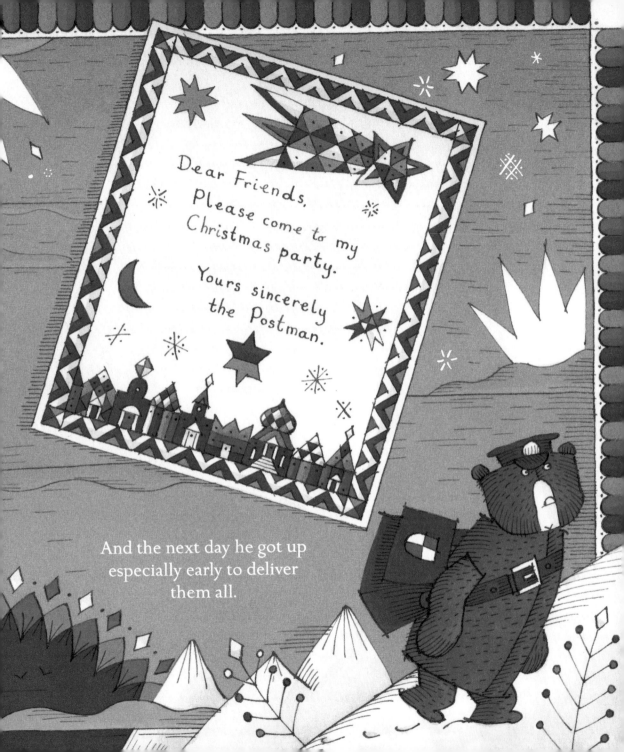

Dear Friends,
Please come to my
Christmas party.

Yours sincerely
the Postman.

And the next day he got up
especially early to deliver
them all.

And that evening he decorated his cave...
and put on a party hat and waited.

And waited...

...AND waited.

And there wasn't a sound, except for the wind.

Well, he thought, after all, who would ever
want to come to *his* Christmas party?
And he hung up his hat and thought that
perhaps it was time for bed.

But then he heard a tweet, and a squeak,
and lots of shy, little voices
saying, "May we come in?"

And there were all the little creatures,
and soon they were all laughing,
and singing and dancing.

And Bear did the silliest dance of all.

And the next day, when he went to work,
he found that all the letters were for him!

He had never seen a letter addressed
to him before.
"I'd better deliver them," he said.

He didn't have a letterbox, or even a door, so he put
the letters in the branches of the tree.

And when he'd hung up his hat and cooked some soup,
he opened them one by one, with great care.

And inside every envelope was a thank you card,
wishing him a very happy Christmas!